T0193750

OH! THOSE CRAZY DOGS!
We're Moving
BOOK TEN
CAL
ILLUSTRATED BY:
RACHAEL PLAQUET

Copyright © 2023 by CAL. 843828

All rights reserved. No part of this book may
be reproduced or transmitted in any form or by
any means, electronic or mechanical, including
photocopying, recording, or by any information
storage and retrieval system, without permission in
writing from the copyright owner.

This is a work of fiction. Names, characters,
places and incidents either are the product of the
author's imagination or are used fictitiously, and any
resemblance to any actual persons, living or dead,
events, or locales is entirely coincidental.

To order additional copies of this book, contact:
Xlibris
844-714-8691
www.Xlibris.com
Orders@Xlibris.com

ISBN: Softcover   978-1-6698-6128-7
       EBook   978-1-6698-6129-4

Print information available on the last page

Rev. date: 12/29/2022

OH! THOSE CRAZY DOGS!

WE'RE MOVING

Introduction

This is a story about 2 crazy dogs, their adventures and the mischief they get into.

They are very loving dogs, but they can't help getting into things.

Hi ! I'm Colby! I'm big and red and furry ! I love everyone but sometimes people are afraid of me because I am so big!

Hi! I'm Teddy Bear! I'm big and white and very furry! I'm not as big as Colby, but just about. Everyone thinks I'm cute and I put shows on for them.

He puts shows on for everyone, rolls on his back and kicks his legs up.

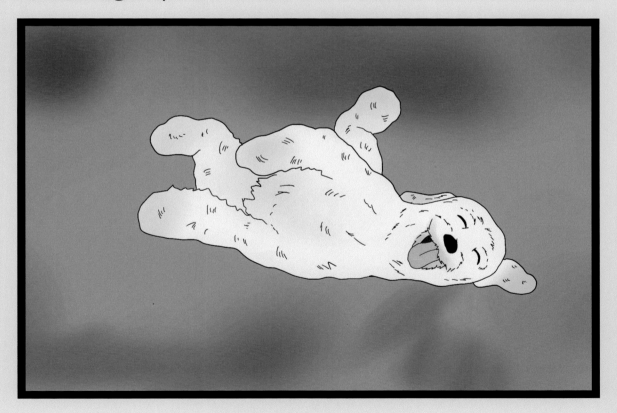

Our owners picked us out specially and brought us home to love and care for us. We love them too, very much. They give us everything and a warm loving home. We will call them Mom and Pop.

Sometimes we don't listen to them, especially me, Teddi Bear!

Our Mom and Pop love us anyway. Sometimes I get Colby in trouble. I can get him to do anything I want because he loves me too and can't say no. He protects me all the time.

WE'RE MOVING!

Colby and Teddi Bear were at the cottage with mom and pop. Something seemed different this time. Mom was putting all her things in boxes and containers. All the kitchen stuff and her pictures and books, their clothes, everything was going into boxes!

Then the dogs noticed the boat was gone! They ran to the lake but no boat! All the beach chairs and umbrella were gone! What was going on?

Colby and Teddi Bear went back up to the cottage and heard some one coming down the driveway. They both started barking which alerted mom and pop that someone was here. A man and a woman in a truck, pulling a trailer.

Mom hugged both of them and Colby and Teddi Bear went to greet them with tails wagging and barking. Everyone sat down in the cottage and had lunch together then the man started putting a whole bunch of mom's boxes and furniture in the trailer! Then the man filled up his truck.

Another man arrived in a truck and a woman in her car. "Wow! Lot's of family here this time!" Teddi Bear said to Colby, "but what are they doing with all of our things!" Pop had brought his big van and mom had driven her van with us in it. We were very confused. All the people took all the boxes and beach furniture and loaded them into all the vehicles.

That night everyone had a big dinner together and talked and laughed. One man left late that night and everyone else slept over. The next morning mom made all the people a big breakfast, washed the dishes and packed them in a box. The two other women were cleaning everywhere. The men were still bringing boxes into the vehicles. Mom even took all the food out of the cupboards and fridge. Nearly everything was gone!

Colby and Teddi Bear tried to stay out of everyone's way but it was hard especially since they were so curious about what was going on. "I don't have a good feeling about this." Teddi Bear said to Colby. "Neither do I" agreed Colby. They would peek around corners and run outside to watch them put the boxes in one of the vehicles.

The pups heard mom ask pop to take us to the lake for our last swim. "Last swim? What does she mean last swim?" asked Teddi Bear. "Oh no!" exclaimed Colby, looking very sad, "I don't think we're coming back to the cottage anymore!" "No! Tell me it isn't true!" cried Teddi Bear, with tears rolling down his face. "Well, there's nothing left here to come back to, just the building!" exclaimed Colby. Colby and Teddi Bear followed pop down to the empty beach and ran into the water. They didn't feel like playing so just stood in the water looking at pop. They were very sad.

Pop brought them back up the stairs to the cottage and dried them off with a towel. Colby and Teddi Bear sat outside drying off and watching everyone putting boxes into their vehicles. It didn't take too much longer before one after the other, cars started leaving.

Teddi Bear looked at Colby then ran back into the cottage. It was empty! He heard mom upstairs and ran up to find her. Mom was making sure everything was locked up but she was crying! Teddi Bear rubbed up against her thigh. He didn't like it when mom was sad. Mom started walking down the stairs and said "Come on Teddi Bear! We have to go now." Teddi Bear ran down the stairs and found Colby sitting near the empty kitchen. Colby looked really sad too! Mom checked to make sure everything was locked down stairs too and in the basement.

Then she grabbed her purse and keys and said "Come on boy's, let's go. Time to go home." We ran out and waited for her by the van door, she locked the cottage door. Then mom did something strange, she leaned her head against the window of the door for a minute then turned, walked down the steps and let us into the van. Colby and Teddi Bear weren't feeling very good about this at all and mom wasn't saying anything. Mom got into her van which was packed full of all kinds of things. She started her van and drove down the driveway.

She told us to say goodbye to the cottage and tears were sliding down her cheeks again. Colby was sitting on the floor beside mom and put his head on her lap. Teddi Bear was sitting in his usual spot, looking out the window at everything. Teddi Bear was concerned about mom too but he was always one happy dog and had to be occupied.

The drive was long as usual and we made our normal stops but this time mom played music all the way home. Sometimes Colby would sit in pops chair and other times he would sit beside mom and put his head on her lap.

We finally arrived home and saw pops truck in the driveway. "Oh good! Pop is home!" exclaimed Teddi Bear. Mom drove into the garage parked her van then let us into the house. We ran upstairs and to the back of the house to the patio doors. Teddi Bear barked so mom or pop could open the door to let us out.

As soon as the door was opened Colby and Teddi Bear
ran and jumped into the pool "Yahoo!" yelled Teddi Bear,
"we still have the pool to swim in!"

Colby did his usual swim around the pool then got out and lay on the patio watching Teddi Bear play. He would get his toy bone and run to the deep end, drop the bone in the pool, then run to the shallow end, down the stairs and jump into the pool. Teddi Bear would swim fast to get his bone then swim back to the shallow end with the toy bone in his mouth, climb up the steps and run to the deep end and drop his bone in again. He would do the whole routine over and over again because mom wasn't there to play with him so Teddi Bear would play by himself!

Colby and Teddi Bear had a good summer playing in the pool with mom and pop would watch. They had a good time but every once in awhile mom would say something strange. "Next year you are going to swim in a great big pool and have a big yard to play in!" We weren't quite sure what she meant.

One day Colby and Teddi Bear were playing in the house when they noticed mom was putting her fancy decorations and pictures and all kinds of stuff in boxes again! Colby and Teddi Bear looked at each other and yelled "No!" They ran around mom and barked at her. Mom kept telling us to go and play because she was busy.

This house was much larger than the cottage and had a lot more things in it and it still had all the stuff from the cottage stored in the basement. Mom kept packing and one of the ladies who came to the cottage to help pack came to our home to help pack there. Then another one of the women came and helped pop, then one of the men who was at the cottage came to help pop. "Oh noo!" cried Teddi Bear, those people made our cottage go away and now they're going to make our home go away!" "I don't think they made anything go away Teddi Bear," said Colby, "I think they just come to help mom and pop. I've heard mom and pop talking. They were talking about when they sold the cottage, which means someone bought it from them.

Then I heard mom and pop talking about selling this house." "Oh no!" cried Teddi Bear. "Then where are we going to live?" asked Teddi Bear. "I don't know" replied Colby, "but I don't like this moving thing!". The packed boxes were piling up all over the house. They still had their dog toy box though but there was getting to be less room to play in the house because of all the boxes.

"Oh Colby, Colby, what is going to happen to us? What are we going to do?" cried Teddi Bear and he ran to his bed and stayed there. Colby went to his bed too because there was nothing to do and he thought he would keep Teddi Bear company. They both just lay there and watched everyone go back and forth, up and down, in and out, up and down. They were so busy for weeks.

Then one day two very large trucks pulled up outside of the house and a whole bunch of men came into the house and started taking all of our boxes and furniture out and putting them in the big trucks. Mom sat with us in a chair in the big empty family room all day while the men worked.

It was late at night when all the trucks and cars drove away. We were left in an empty house with mom and pop. Mom got up and went to the fridge and pop to the freezer downstairs. They had coolers to put the food into and filled them all up, then put them in mom and pop's vans. "Come on Colby and Teddi Bear, let's go. Say goodbye to your old home because we're going to your new home now!" "Our new home?" asked Teddi Bear, "I don't want to leave my home! What about my swimming pool? Are they bringing that with them?" "No Teddi Bear, they can't bring the swimming pool.

Maybe there will be one at the new place. It was very dark and very late as they drove for a long time. You would think they were going to the cottage, but it's the wrong way!" said Teddi Bear. Finally, after a long and very dark ride, there weren't any lights on the streets here or houses. Mom turned into a driveway that was all dark. She kept her lights on so pop could find her.

Pop finally drove into the driveway and put us into a fenced yard so we were safe and then went into the house and turned lights on so everyone could see. "Wow this yard is huge! Colby and Teddi Bear ran all over checking everything out. There were a couple of decks and gardens, the yard was all grass. "There's no pool" said Teddi sadly. "No, but I can smell water Teddi" said Colby, "we'll have to wait until we can see in the morning to find out what it is."

Mom called them in and Teddi Bear and Colby ran up the deck stairs and through some patio doors and into a kitchen. "Wow! This is nice!" exclaimed Teddi Bear, "but where is all our furniture?" "I heard mom talking to pop about the trucks coming in tomorrow morning so I guess they're bringing everything then" "Where are they going to sleep?" asked Teddi Bear.

"I don't know" replied Colby. Pop went outside to his van and brought in two air mattresses, then put air in them with an electric pump. Mom and pop were so tired, they finished putting the cold food in the fridge and freezers and just fell on the air mattresses with their clothes on. Colby and Teddi Bear lay down on the floor beside them and fell asleep too.

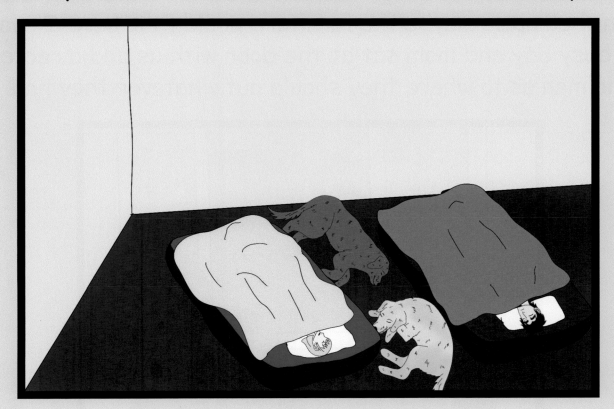

In the morning, two large trucks pulled up in the new driveway. The driveway was long and the 2 trucks fit in it along with mom and pops vans. They pulled up near the front door and started bringing all our things in the house! This house was smaller than the last one and only one floor instead of stairs everywhere! This was much better for mom! But the basement was like another house! It was all finished up so maybe the furniture would fit in here! It was a busy day and mom sat at the door with us and directed the men as to where they should put whatever they had.

We were allowed to go out into the yard whenever we wanted and the first time we went out, we found where the water smell was coming from. Our house was on a huge lake! We couldn't even see the end of it or a shore anywhere. Mom and pop had fenced in the back yard so we couldn't go down the stairs to the lake without them. We couldn't go down to the beach alone because this lake was very different and had huge waves but the colour was beautiful and kept changing. That never happened at the cottage. Even the cottage yard wasn't this wide!

"Where's the pool? cried Teddi Bear?" "You don't need a pool, we have a great big lake right there!" replied Colby. "Yes, but I can't go in it anytime I want and I can't play with my toys like I used to. It was all about playing" said Teddi Bear. "Oh Teddi Bear, it will work out for you, I'm sure. Mom and pop spent many days unpacking and placing their furniture where they wanted it.

There was still a lot of stuff in the basement. They bought two more large beds for the bedrooms downstairs and all kinds of patio furniture and a dining set for outside and a huge umbrella. She filled in some corners with planters that we had to fill in when it was warmer.

There wasn't any snow here though, there should be at this time of year. But we weren't going to get any. We had moved south of where we had lived before and it wasn't usually cold enough for snow. "Maybe sometimes" mom said. "This is really hard" said Teddi Bear, "we won't get snow here to play in, we don't have the cottage anymore, we don't have our home anymore, mom and pop are too tired to play with us and I don't know what to do. All our friends are gone, there aren't any houses here to find new friends. What are we going to do Colby?" cried Teddi Bear.

"We are going to be just fine Teddi Bear." replied Colby. "Look at all the yard we can play in! There's a big double deck we can sit on with mom and pop, there's the lake when we're allowed, pop can play ball and throw the ball as far as he can and you can run really fast to catch it. We can have fun here and mom and pop are home all the time now!"

As mom and pop unpacked, Teddi Bear and Colby would play outside by them selves. When they were outside, they began to notice a lot of wildlife. Teddi Bear kept finding bunnies and would chase them as fast as he could. The bunnies would slip under the fence and get away but it was still fun for Teddi Bear. There were so many kinds of birds. Small ones, large birds, colourful birds, butterflies.

They all came to eat from pop's feeders. They saw raccoons and possums, fox and groundhogs, squirrels and other animals that we could smell or hear in the fields in the dark. This was different from where we used to live but very exciting. Teddi Bear would chase everything he could and bark at the ones in the fields. They were actually having a lot of fun, just a different kind of fun.

When mom and pop were finished unpacking all the boxes and setting up the furniture they finally relaxed and sat outside on the deck. They had put the dining table and BBQ and smoker on the upper level and the couch and more tables and chairs and planters and lots of things on the lower deck. It was very big. Mom and pop would throw balls for us and when it got warm out, they planted some gardens.

One day pop unlocked the gate in front of the stairs that led down to the lake. "O boy!" exclaimed Teddi Bear, "we're going down to the lake!" Colby and Teddi Bear ran down the stairs and went to jump into the lake but stopped in the sand. The waves coming in were huge, way over their heads!

Colby and Teddi Bear slowly walked into the shallow water but another one of those big waves was coming right at them. They both stood there and the wave knocked them over and they rolled up to the shoreline. "I don't think I like that" complained Teddi Bear.

The lake looked so beautiful but today it was very rough. Both dogs turned around and started walking up the stairs. "Hey boy's" said pop, "where are you going?" Mom looked at the huge waves and said "I don't think they like the waves. We'll have to bring them down when the lake is calmer." Mom and pop followed the pups up the stairs to the yard and pop locked the gate behind them.

"Well, that was different." said Colby. We should sit with mom and pop on the deck and dry off in the sun. The dogs lay down and mom got up, went into the house and brought out some treats for everyone. It really was a beautiful day, the sun was shining, the birds were singing, mom and pop were chatting and Teddi Bear was on the alert for any animal that dared to come around our yard. He loved to chase everything. Colby lay his head down and went to sleep.

The dogs did get down to the lake when it was calm but unfortunately that didn't happen very often. When they did go they really enjoyed themselves. The water was cool and refreshing. It was a beautiful blue/green colour and they could walk out a long way.

Pop would throw the balls for each of them and they would swim real fast to get their ball. If Teddi Bear caught his ball first, he would swim as fast as he could to try to catch Colby's but Colby knew what he was up to and would swim faster to catch his ball. It was a lot of fun.

In the fall there were leaves falling everywhere. That was fun too! Pop would pile them up for us and we would run right through them. We had a lot of trees on the property so it was easy to make a pile.

One day we were sitting on the deck and we started noticing a lot of butterflies flying past. More and more every day for nearly a week. It was so beautiful! Mom said they were migrating.

Then we had hundreds of blue jays that stopped for a few days in the trees in the front yard. It was magnificent when they all flew out of the trees at the same time.

Then we saw dozens of eagles flying together, then many, many other very big black birds all flying together. They were all flying the same way, south.

It was starting to get a bit colder now and we found this refreshing because of our long hair. We couldn't wait for the snow to come, but it didn't, except for a couple of times and we couldn't even make a snowbank or snuffle in the snow. Pop didn't even have to shovel it.

So Colby and Teddi Bear would go out and walk all over the yard looking for trespassing animals and chase them. One day Colby and Teddi Bear were sitting on the deck when a raccoon popped his head up from the hill. Teddi Bear was going to run at him but Colby told him to wait. "Let's see what it does." They watched the raccoon approach the bird feeders. There were two close together and the raccoon decided to try to climb the two poles to get to the seed. He grabbed onto the first pole with on front foot and one back foot, then did the same with the second pole. He slowly made his way up the slippery poles until he reached the bird feeders hanging from the hooks. When he would try to reach the feeder with his front foot he would slide down the pole a bit. So, the raccoon used one back foot to grab onto a feeder and then his other back foot to grab onto the other feeder.

Now what? He looked puzzled. He couldn't let go of the poles. Slowly his back feet started to split apart because the raccoon couldn't hold the position. He ended up doing the splits and still hanging on to the feeders. He was really stuck. Colby and Teddi Bear were laughing so hard!

Slowly the raccoon started to slide down the pole and flipped over which made his back feet release from the feeders. He fell to the ground and decided to eat the seed that had fallen beneath the feeders. The dogs didn't see the raccoon do that again, he always ate the seed from the ground.

The little raccoon visited every day and the dogs got used to him being there so Teddi Bear didn't bother chasing him anymore. They got used to their new life and began to really enjoy it. Living here was like living at the cottage but it was all the time. Mom called it a perma-cottage. The dogs loved their new home but what made it the best was that all four of them were together.

Thank you for reading the 'Oh! Those Crazy Dog's!' series. We appreciate your interest in the dog's adventures and hope they have added some joy to your day. These stories were based on the activities of two real dogs, golden doodles, with some added storytelling to make it more interesting. The two dogs really are crazy, very active and make the author laugh every day, usually within a few minutes of getting up in the morning. Colby and Teddi Bear continue to enjoy their lives while surprising us with their intelligent behavior. We hope you enjoyed these books.

Books in the "Oh Those Crazy Dogs"
Series by author **CAL**

Book one	Colby Comes Home
Book two	Teddi Bear Comes Home
Book three	Teddi Bear's First Time at the Lake!
Book four	A New Friend In The Neighbourhood! DIGGER!
Book five	Teddi Bear and Colby Love Swimming in the Pool
Book six	Colby and Teddi Bear Go To The Circus
Book seven	Tyse Comes To Visit
Book eight	Winter Fun
Book nine	Fun At The Cottage – Winter and Summer
Book ten	We're Moving!

Printed in the United States
by Baker & Taylor Publisher Services